This Jake book
belongs to . .

. . . .

Also by Simon James

The Day Jake Vacuumed

Jake and the Babysitter

For Norman, my friend – and my accountant, with love

Copyright © 1994 Simon James

First published 1994 by Macmillan Children's Books, an imprint of Macmillan Publishers Limited a division of Macmillan Limited Cavaye Place London SW10 9PG and Basingstoke Associated companies throughout the world

This edition published 1995

9 8 7 6 5 4 3 2 1

ISBN 0 333 62957 4

Printed in Hong Kong

With warm thanks to Sian for photography

Jake
and his cousin
Sidney

Jake's Dad

Jake

and his cousin
Sidney

Simon James

MACMILLAN CHILDREN'S BOOKS

Jake didn't like babies. All they seemed
to do was cry and smell something awful.
So you can imagine how Jake felt one
day when he had to look after his
cousin Sidney.

Jake changed Sidney's nappy and then
tried to feed him, but it wasn't long
before Sidney needed a bath.

Jake carried Sidney upstairs to the
bathroom and turned on the taps. The
bath always took such a long time to fill.
So Jake thought he would go to his
bedroom and read for a while.
Sidney waited.

And he waited.
In fact it really was quite some time
before Jake remembered Sidney's bath.
He rushed out of his bedroom towards
the bathroom door…

…only to find Sidney floating out on the crest of a gigantic wave.
"Don't cry, Sidney! Be brave!" shouted Jake, as together they

shot the rapids downstairs to the hall.

Meanwhile, in the lounge, Jake's father began to wonder what all the slurping noise was outside in the hallway. He got up from his chair and went towards the door.

Jake and Sidney, meanwhile, were beginning to wonder just how much MORE water would fill the hall.

Fortunately, Jake's father opened the door – and was immediately engulfed by a huge tidal wave of frothy bath water. "Hooray!" said Jake.

As the house filled with water, Jake's sister was on her way home from Brownies. She'd just reached the house when

out burst an enormous tidal wave containing her parents, assorted bits of furniture and, of course, right at the top, Jake and his cousin Sidney.

Jake's parents stood helplessly and stared as their beautiful home, now filled to the brim with water, slowly lifted from its foundations and started to float down the road.

That night Jake's father had to book the whole family into the local hotel. He made sure that Jake and Sidney had to share the same room.

But Jake didn't mind looking after his brave cousin Sidney. And Sidney certainly didn't cry any more.
He knew…

…he'd grow up to be just like Jake.

love from
Jake and Sidney

Other Macmillan picture books you will enjoy

FLEA'S BEST FRIEND   Charles Fuge
BLOOP AND THE BIG BAD BARONS   Peter Haswell
TACKY THE PENGUIN   Helen Lester / Lynn Munsinger
GRUMPY NICOLA   Kara May / Doffy Weir
MARTHA SPEAKS   Susan Meddaugh
MY GRAMPA'S GOT BIG POCKETS   Selina Young

For a complete list of titles, write to

Macmillan Children's Books
18–21 Cavaye Place
London SW10 9PG